THIS WALKER BOOK BELONGS TO:

_____

_____

_____

_____

red nose readers

Fee Fi Fo Fum

Allan Ahlberg
Colin McNaughton

The Pie
Cat + Fish
Fee Fi Fo Fum

WALKER BOOKS
AND SUBSIDIARIES
LONDON • BOSTON • SYDNEY

First published 1985 by
Walker Books Limited
87 Vauxhall Walk
London SE11 5HJ

This edition published 1990
Reprinted 1993, 1994, 1996, 1999

Text © 1985 Allan Ahlberg
Illustrations © 1985 Colin McNaughton

Printed in Hong Kong

British Library Cataloguing in Publication Data
A catalogue record for this book is
available from the British Library.

ISBN 0-7445-1499-1

The Pie

Who made the pie?

Who stole the pie?

Who looked for the pie?

Who found the pie?

Who ate the pie?

They did!

Who washed up?

Cat + Fish

flower + bee = honey

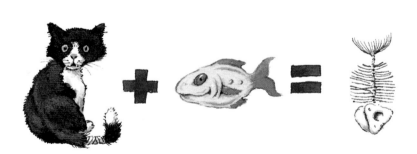

cat + fish = bones

cow + grass = milk

rain + sun = rainbow

baby + bag = mess

Fee Fi Fo Fum

sun

house

girl

boy

giant's
castle

giant's mum

↑ giant's dad

giant

giant's
dog

the end

red nose readers